A Note to

Welcome to REAL KIDS READERS, a series of phonics-based books for children who are beginning to read. In the classroom, educators use phonics to teach children how to sound out unfamiliar words, providing a firm foundation for reading skills. At home, you can use REAL KIDS READERS to reinforce and build on that foundation, because the books follow the same basic phonic guidelines that children learn in school.

Of course the best way to help your child become a good reader is to make the experience fun—and REAL KIDS READERS do that, too. With their realistic story lines and lively characters, the books engage children's imaginations. With their clean design and sparkling photographs, they provide picture clues that help new readers decipher the text. The combination is sure to entertain young children and make them truly want to read.

REAL KIDS READERS have been developed at three distinct levels to make it easy for children to read at their own pace.

- LEVEL 1 is for children who are just beginning to read.
- LEVEL 2 is for children who can read with help.
- LEVEL 3 is for children who can read on their own.

A controlled vocabulary provides the framework at each level. Repetition, rhyme, and humor help increase word skills. Because children can understand the words and follow the stories, they quickly develop confidence. They go back to each book again and again, increasing their proficiency and sense of accomplishment, until they're ready to move on to the next level. The result is a rich and rewarding experience that will help them develop a lifelong love of reading.

To Bridget and Michal,
who can read this now. It's easy!
—M. B.

Special thanks to
Hanna Andersson, Portland, OR, for supplying clothing.

Produced by DWAI / Seventeenth Street Productions, Inc.

Library of Congress Cataloging-in-Publication Data

Bernstein, Margery.
 That's hard, that's easy / by Margery Bernstein ; photography by Dorothy Handelman.
  p.   cm. — (Real kids readers. Level 2)
 Summary: A child notices that things that were once difficult to do often become easy as people grow.
 ISBN 0-7613-2007-5 (lib. bdg.). — ISBN 0-7613-2032-6 (pbk.)
 [1. Growth—Fiction. 2. Stories in rhyme.] I. Handelman, Dorothy, ill. II. Title. III. Series.
PZ8.3.B45854Th 1998
[E]—dc21
                                                    97-31373
                                                    CIP
                                                    AC

pbk: 10 9 8 7 6 5 4 3 2 1
lib: 10 9 8 7 6 5 4 3 2 1

That's Hard, That's Easy

Margery Bernstein

Photographs by **Dorothy Handelman**

M

The Millbrook Press

Brookfield, Connecticut

There are things I cannot do.
I cannot make a pie, can you?
That's hard for me.

But there are things that I *can* do.
I climb up stairs and jump down too.
That's easy for me.

My brother Jake is very small.
It's hard for him to hold a ball.
He drops it.

He cannot play an easy game.
He cannot even say his name.
It's hard for him.

He cannot walk. He can't stand up.
He cannot hold a spoon or cup.
We have to help him.

We cannot keep this baby neat.
What a mess when he tries to eat!
It's hard for him.

I could not do most things at all
when I was very, very small.
But now I can.

Now I am big and I can do
all the things that Jake wants to.
It's easy for me.

I can hop and I can bop.
I can dance until I drop.
It's fun.

I can sing and I can hum.
I can even play a drum.
It's easy.

I'll make you lunch. Do you like ham?
Or how about some bread and jam?
I'll get it.

I'll send a card to Gram and Gramp.
I wrote my name. Now where's a stamp?
I'll find one.

When I was small, about Jake's age,
I could not draw or read a page.
Now I can.

But there are things I still can't do.
I cannot fly a kite, can you?
That's hard.

I want to skate. I want to spin.
But when I try, my feet turn in.
One day I'll learn.

I'd like to dive into the pool
just like the big kids. They look cool.
One day I will.

My dad can paint and play a horn.
He fixed my pants when they were torn.
He said it was easy.

My mom plays chess. She bakes us bread.
She made the quilt that's on my bed.
She said it was easy.

When I get big these things will be
as easy for me as A, B, C.
I hope.

Yes, they will be as easy for me
as playing ball or climbing a tree.
I think.

One thing I know. It's really true.
What's hard for me
may be easy for you.

And I can also plainly see
what's hard for you
may be easy for me.

Phonic Guidelines
Use the following guidelines to help your child read the words in *That's Hard, That's Easy.*

Short Vowels
When two consonants surround a vowel, the sound of the vowel is usually short. This means you pronounce *a* as in apple, *e* as in egg, *i* as in igloo, *o* as in octopus, and *u* as in umbrella. Short-vowel words in this story include: *bed, big, bop, but, can, cup, Dad, get, ham, him, his, hop, hum, jam, kids, Mom, not, yes.*

Consonant Blends
When two or more different consonants are side by side, they usually blend to make a com bined sound. In this story, words with consonant blends include: *bread, draw, drop, drum, Gram, Gramp, help, hold, jump, just, most, pants, send, spin, stamp, stand, wants.*

Double Consonants
When two identical consonants appear side by side, one of them is silent. Double-consonant words in this story include: *chess, mess, small, still, will,* and words in the *all* family: *all, ball.*

R-Controlled Vowels
When a vowel is followed by the letter *r*, its sound is changed by the *r*. In this story, words with r-controlled vowels include: *are, card, for, hard, horn, torn, turn.*

Long Vowel and Silent E
If a word has a vowel and ends with an *e*, usually the vowel is long and the *e* is silent. Long vowels are pronounced the same way as their alphabet names. In this story, words with a long vowel and silent *e* include: *age, bakes, dive, game, Jake, kite, like, made, make, name, page, skate, wrote.*

Double Vowels
When two vowels are side by side, usually the first vowel is long and the second vowel is silent. Double-vowel words in this story include: *day, eat, keep, may, neat, paint, pie, play, read, say, see, tree, tries.*

Diphthongs
Sometimes when two vowels (or a vowel and a consonant) are side by side, they combine to make a diphthong—a sound that is different from long or short vowel sounds. Diphthongs are: *au, aw, ew, oi, oy, ou, ow.* In this story, words with diphthongs include: *down, how, now.*

Consonant Digraphs
Sometimes when two different consonants are side by side, they make a digraph that represents a single new sound. Consonant digraphs are: *ch, sh, th, wh.* In this story, words with digraphs include: *chess, lunch, that, there, these, they, things, think, when, where.*

Silent Consonants
Sometimes when two different consonants are side by side, one of them is silent. In this story, words with silent consonants include: *climb, walk.*

Sight Words
Sight words are those words that a reader must learn to recognize immediately—by sight—instead of by sounding them out. They occur with high frequency in easy texts. Sight words not included in the above categories are: *a, am, an, and, as, at, be, cool, could, do, easy, even, have, he, I, in, is, it, look, my, one, said, the, to, too, up, us, very, was, we, were, you.*